Wheedleneeps the Brownie

Written by Sandy McKnight

Illustrated by Shalla Gray

Curlytale Books

To Grey Galloway,
where heart and mind found rest.
Sandy, July 2018

For my wee black dog,
waiting in Summerlands
Shalla, July 2018

Wheedleneeps McTumshie was a Brownie and a very naughty one too. I daresay you think his name is unusual, and I don't suppose you have many friends called that.

Wheedleneeps' name came from his liking for turnips, which in Scotland are called neeps. He would beg, borrow, steal or wheedle them.

3

 heedleneeps loved turnips.

He loved them boiled;

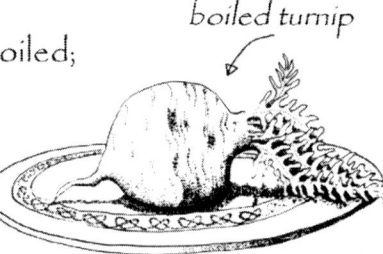
boiled turnip

He loved them roasted;

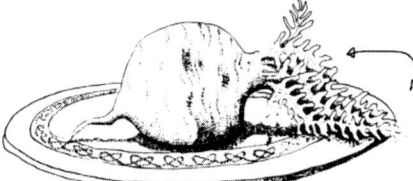
roasted turnip

He loved them raw;

raw turnip
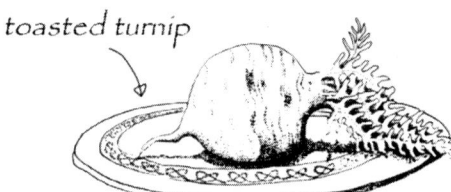

toasted turnip

He loved them toasted.

But the ones he liked best were stolen.

stolen turnip
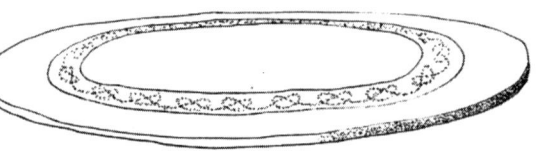

"Stolen neeps, nice and sweet.
Them that loses them can greet"

That's what he told his friends and anyone
who tried to tell him what he was
doing was wrong.

he stole neeps from gardens, from allotments and from farmers' fields. When he heard Farmer Mack was going to plant a whole field full, Wheedleneeps was delighted.

"A whole field of neeps and just for me!" he cried; "Hundreds and thousands of neeps!"

He was so happy he burst into song:

"Neeps, neeps,

Planted deep

Up in the field

with sides so

steep.

Some for dinner and

some for tea,

And yet there's only

enough for me!"

ell, Farmer Mack planted his field and weeks went past.

Every day Farmer Mack went out to see how his neeps were
growing and every night Wheedleneeps did the same.
Before long, Wheedleneeps thought,
"These neeps are as big as golf balls, and that's big
enough for me to eat."

So he went out and he stole ten turnips.

When Farmer Mack saw the empty spaces in his field where his turnips had been, he was angry. "That's them rabbits what's eating them", he said. He went home and got his dog Snaffle and shot three rabbits dead.

All the animals were sad at what had happened but Wheedleneeps just laughed.

"Serves them right", he said, "They shouldn't be so daft as to sit around when Farmer Mack's on the prowl".

he next night and the next again Wheedleneeps took even more turnips and he ate them all. When Farmer Mack saw more turnips had gone he said: "That's Loppylugs the Hare that's doing this. I bet them rabbits told him where to find my turnips." The next day when Loppylugs was on his way to a nice field full of clover Farmer Mack was waiting for him.

Suddenly there was a loud BANG! Farmer Mack had shot Loppylugs the Hare dead. That night Farmer Mack cooked and ate Loppylugs with some boiled turnips.

Now the animals were really angry. They went to Wheedleneeps' house and Two Stripes the Badger said to him: "You have to stop stealing Farmer Mack's turnips.

Innocent creatures are dying because of you."

Wheedleneeps was quiet for a moment, and then he laughed.

9

"h ha ha ha!" he said, "hee, hee, hee! Silly old hare!"

and he sang; *"Hare, hare, doesn't care,*

> *For he has gone away somewhere,*

> *Down the valley, up the hill*

> *And Farmer Mack's sure had his fill!"*

All the animals were horrified and, although the weasels tittered

a bit, that was because they were nervous and a little frightened.

This was getting out of hand.

That night
Wheedleneeps stole an
even bigger bagful
of turnips.

go away

He stole so many he could hardly carry them all
home and then he couldn't get them all into his
house. Farmer Mack was furious when he saw how
many neeps were gone.

11

"It's them pigeons that's eating them," he said.

"I bet that hare told them where to get them."

Next morning, just as the dawn came and the sun came up, Farmer Mack appeared in Knockbreck Wood with his shotgun and killed four Woodpigeons. That night he had them for his tea.

He thought that by eating them he was getting his own back...

but he wasn't, was he?

12

The animals were enraged, and called a full council meeting, known as a moot. Some called it a Hootmoot for Taw Knee the owl, the council leader, was the oldest and wisest creature of them all.

13

"**T**his has gone far enough" said Two Stripes the

Badger, "something must be done about Wheedleneeps."

"But what are we to do?" asked Mrs Prickleskin the Hedgehog,

"He just laughs at us all."

"Yes, I met him this morning after Farmer Mack had shot the

cushats," said Squatter the Toad, "and I gave him a piece of

my mind. He just laughed and sang:

"Pigeons dead they cannot fly
And neither can a pigeon pie.

I've neeps for breakfast and neeps for tea,
And Farmer Mack he don't scare me!"

I was so disgusted that I spat at him

and hopped away,"

said the unhappy toad.

14

"That's the trouble," said Littlemouse the Bat, who hung upside down on the oak tree; Nothing seems to scare him. I don't think he's afraid of anything or anyone."

Taw Knee's eyes were closed. He opened them and holding up a wing for everyone to be quiet, he said in a very stern voice, "I know who he is afraid of."

"Whoo? Whoo?" said the Little Owls

"Who? Who?" squeaked the Field Mice.

"Who? Who?" croaked Squatter.

15

Everybody clamoured to hear who could frighten Wheedleneeps. When the noise had died down Taw Knee said in a quiet voice, "I believe it is time to call on Herne the Hunter."

There was a great gasp from all the animals gathered there. Some of the little ones even cried out in fright; Herne the Hunter, the name was magical. Herne was the God of All the Greenwood, the most powerful being in all the Universe, and he rode a horse that blew fire and flames from his nostrils.

Herne the Hunter.

Even Two Stripes the Badger shivered at the sound of that name; not that Herne was evil, it was just that he was so powerful.

"I believe this is what we must do," said Taw Knee and gradually, as they discussed it, more and more of the animals agreed that it was the only way.

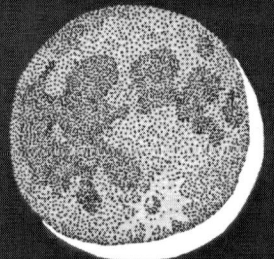

"ut how do we do it?" asked Brushtail the Fox. "Who knows how to find Herne the Hunter?"

"We will call him to us" said Taw Knee. "We will light a great fire and we will sing and chant and ask him to appear and help us."

It was arranged that they would all meet in the forest clearing at midnight the following day and that everyone would bring some wood for the fire.

That being decided everyone went home by the light of a shiny New Moon and soon all were asleep.

18

The next day Wheedleneeps heard from the weasels about the Council Moot. Wheedleneeps laughed. "Was it to make me their leader?" he asked. "No," said Wily the Weasel. "They are going to get Herne the Hunter to stop your stealing and lying."

"Ain't no such person," said Wheedleneeps, "and I'm not scared of ghosts and bogles." He sang:

"Herne, Herne is very stern,
Frightens fools and silly bairns.
He's never been seen by me or you.
I don't think it's even true."

Wily wasn't so sure - and he certainly didn't want Herne to think that he'd helped make up the song. He ran away and hid.

Just before midnight all the animals were gathered in a great ring in the glade, the smallest on the inside and the tallest on the outside, that way everyone could see what was going on.

At 12 o'clock exactly Taw Knee the owl said, "We must light the fire now."

When the fire was lit, Taw Knee said, "Now we must dance in a great ring and circle the fire. You must clap your paws, stamp your feet and you must squeak, snort, croak, whistle, grunt, sing or howl."

No-one had ever seen or heard such a thing.

Hundreds of animals and birds circling and dancing under the moon by the light of a great fire. Even Wheedleneeps heard them. "What a waste of breath, what a load of great puddings they all are! It's time I fetched some turnips."

21

At the clearing the fire was getting bigger and burning brighter and brighter. The animals were going faster and faster round it and the clapping and singing was getting more and more excited. This is what they chanted:

"O Great Lord Herne from woodland green,

Come, come, come.

From bracken slopes of growing fern,

Come, come, come.

Fire, water, earth and air,

We know you are at hand

Somewhere.

Great Lord, show us

That you care,

Come, come, come."

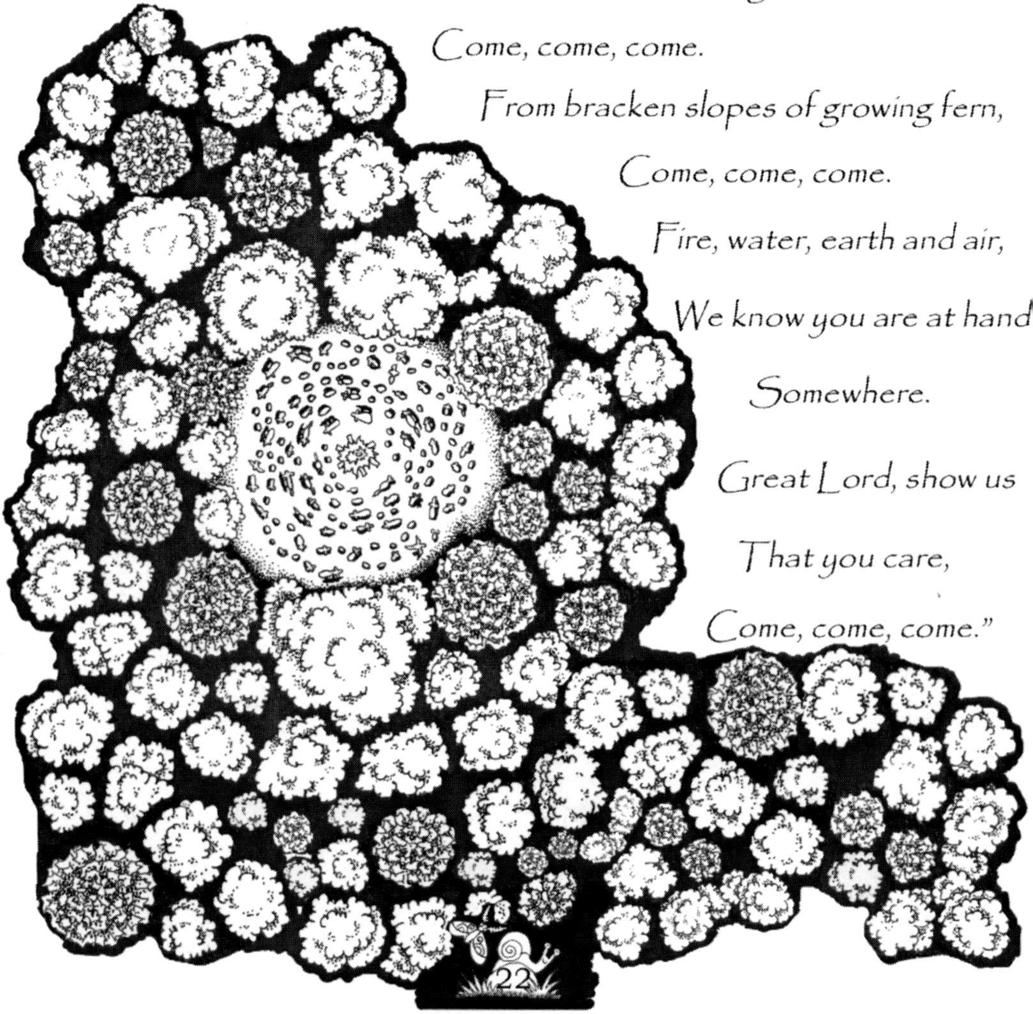

Then, out of nowhere, a bank of mist rolled from the trees across the clearing and everyone stood still.

The mist was thickest near the fire, then a cool breeze blew through the trees and the mist began to clear a little and...

there he was...

Herne the Hunter!

Some animals hid behind their paws, the little ones hid behind their parents, the weasels tried to hide in a hole in a tree, but most of the animals just stood there with their mouths hanging open and stared.

Lord Herne sat upon a great white horse with blue flames coming from his nostrils. He was very big and powerful, gold bracelets shone upon his arms and he wore a headdress of great stag antlers.

Strangely, when talking of it afterwards, everyone said his cloak was a different colour and they were all right for it was a magic cloak which could change colour when it wanted.

His face was stern yet wise and he looked old and yet young. It was all very confusing.

Then he spoke and his voice was like thunder.

"Who has called me from my sleep?"

"We did." said Taw Knee the owl, "It's about

Wheedleneeps and all the innocent creatures that are dead."

"Ah yes," said Herne, "I know something of this but tell me more."

The animals told him about Wheedleneeps stealing and how

Farmer Mack had shot the creatures and how everyone was sad.

Herne got angry, then

he got angrier.

He banged his staff

upon the ground

and the ground shook.

His horse got angry

and bigger flames

came from his

nostrils.

"Where is Wheedleneeps now?" asked Herne.

"Out stealing turnips again." said Brushtail the Fox.

"Then it's time I paid him and Farmer Mack a visit." said Lord Herne. He waved his staff around his head three times and he was gone, vanished, disappeared. No noise, no hoof beats, just...gone!

Pandemonium broke loose as a thousand animals squeaked, squawked, yowled, howled and growled. It was the noisiest the wood had ever been. It was bedlam.

It was so loud Farmer Mack heard it as he lay in his bed. "*I wonder what in the name of goodness has got into those animals!*" he said to himself, and he put his head under the pillow to drown out the noise.

omeone else heard it too. Wheedleneeps was returning home with another bag of stolen turnips. In fact he was in the lane that led directly to his house.

As he got nearer he thought; "That's strange, I can see a flickering blue light. Whatever can it be?"

As to the noise coming from the wood, Wheedleneeps said to himself; "You'd think they'd be in bed by this time. They should be, all of them."

Wheedleneeps walked on a bit further. "How odd!" he thought. "That looks a bit like a horse...with a big person on it. He was beginning to feel a little bit uneasy now.

"Wheedleneeps!" said a loud voice, "I want to speak to you."

"Who are you?" said the Brownie. "Are you a ghost?"

"I am Herne the Hunter." said the voice. "Lord of the Woodland and all its animals."

"I'll just be off then." said Wheedleneeps, and he turned to walk away. Herne lifted up his staff and pointed it. A ring of silver light sprang from it and wrapped itself around Wheedleneeps' legs. He couldn't move.

"hat do you want?" Wheedleneeps shouted, "I've done nothing wrong."

"Nothing?" said Lord Herne. "NOTHING? You have caused the deaths of innocent creatures and you call that nothing!"

"That was Farmer Mack not me." said Wheedleneeps, "I didn't shoot them, he did."

"Because you stole his turnips," said Herne. "And after the animals told you, you did it again and then you laughed at their fate."

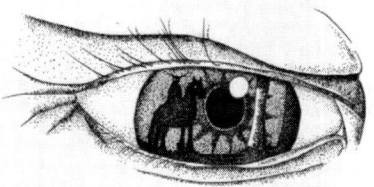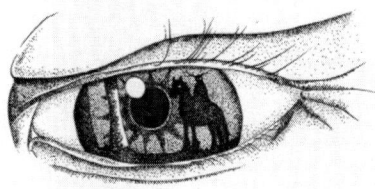

"Ah, they were only mangy rabbits," said Wheedleneeps. "And a mouldy old hare and some noisy pigeons. Who cares?"

"I care!" thundered Herne. "I care for all the animals of this land and all their lives are sacred to me. Your life however, is forfeit and the animals wish to see you punished and justice done."

heedleneeps had heard enough. He dropped his turnips and turned to run back up the lane.

He couldn't move. The silver ring held him fast.

"For your lies, you must pay." said Herne.

Wheedleneeps' feet went cold.

"For your pride, you must pay." said Herne.

Wheedleneeps' knees went cold.

For your stealing, you must pay." said Herne.

Wheedleneeps' tummy went cold.

32

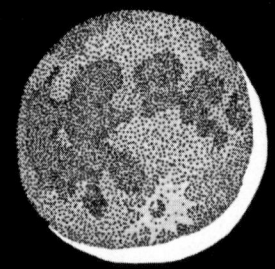

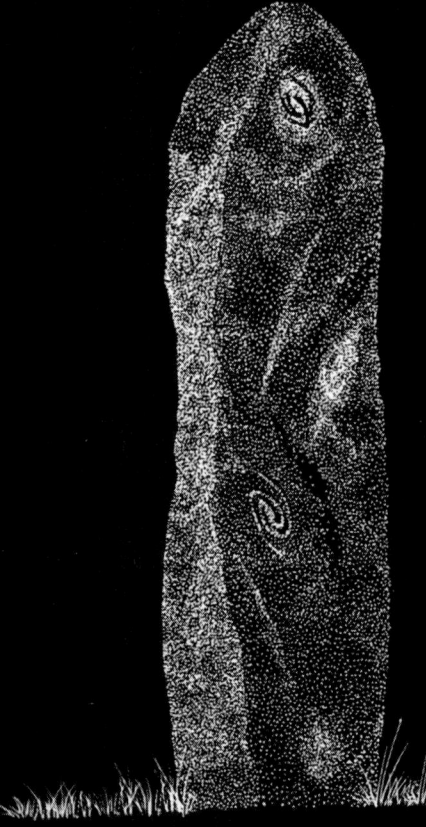

"ut most of all, for allowing others to take the blame

and lose their lives for your dishonesty, for that Wheedleneeps

I give you stone for bone."

And that was it. Wheedleneeps was gone, and in his place stood

a block of stone the same height as he had been.

Herne sighed and patted his horse. "Come Blueflame," he said.

"We have another call to make."

armer Mack was not sleeping at all well. He was already regretting having shot the animals and pigeons.

He was having a nightmare in which he was watching a large horse with a strange rider approaching him. The horse had blue flames playing around his nostrils and the rider had horns on his head.

"No!" thought Farmer Mack, "not horns, antlers! Like a great deer."

Lord Herne spoke to him; "Farmer Mack climb up on Blueflame, there are things I must show you."

Unwillingly, unhappily, Farmer Mack did as he was told and they flew up into the air.

How far or how long they flew, Farmer Mack had no way of knowing for he kept his eyes shut most of the time and he held on for dear life.

hen all motion stopped and he plucked up the courage to open his eyes and look around him. What he saw he would never forget. He was in a beautiful meadow which seemed to go on for mile after mile after mile. There were thousands of flowers of every kind and green trees that waved friendly branches. Through the fields ran a stream of the clearest water Farmer Mack had ever seen. There were bees and butterflies and animals of every kind.

"Where am I?" he asked.

"Summerlands" said Herne. "The home of the animals' spirits when they die. Here they can live in everlasting peace and harmony."

"**T**hen why does that hare look so lonely?" asked Farmer Mack.

"That is the hare you shot because you thought it stole your turnips."

"It did," said Farner Mack.

"No it did not," said Herne, "Wheedleneeps the Brownie did."

"You mean I shot an innocent creature?" said Farmer Mack. "That makes me very unhappy."

"There's more to see," said Herne "Look over there."

38

hen Farmer Mack looked it was to see the three

rabbits he had shot.

"Did they not steal
my turnips?" he said.

"No they did not,"
said Herne

"Again it was Wheedleneeps the Brownie."

"He has a lot to answer for" said Farmer Mack.

"And he has," said Herne, "he has."

Farmer Mack listened.

"How lovely the woodpigeons

croon," he said. "I wish they

could croon

like that in

Knockbreck

Wood."

"They once

did," said Herne.

"You shot them in your temper and your anger."

39

Farmer Mack was very sorry now and the tears ran down his face.

"What can I do?" he cried. "What can I do?"

"I will tell you on the way back," said Lord Herne, "for now we must leave this place. And do not worry. All here are happy. Here they meet and greet their own families and kind, for all are called here in time."

40

ll Farmer Mack could remember of the journey
back was that they rode along a rainbow!
In Knockbreck Wood few saw the rainbow that arched across
the sky at dawn, but Taw Knee the owl did. He blinked and
watched for a moment.
"I think our problems may be over," he said to himself. "We'll
just have to wait and see."

41

Farmer Mack woke early that morning, had breakfast and went into town. There he sold his gun. "I'll never shoot another living creature," he said. "Never! Never! Never!"

Next he went to the seed shop. When he came out he had packets and packets of seeds.

That day he ploughed and planted and all the next day he did the same. The animals were curious that Farmer Mack was acting differently.

And do you know what he had done?

McGillicuddy's Celebrated SEEDS

CARROT

LETTUCE

PEAS

McGillicuddy's

Gillicuddy

McGillicuddy's

e'd planted a field that he called the Broth Field.
There were rows of peas, carrots, beans, lettuce, potatoes,
cabbage, Brussels sprouts and celery...and all of it was for
the animals, every single bit.

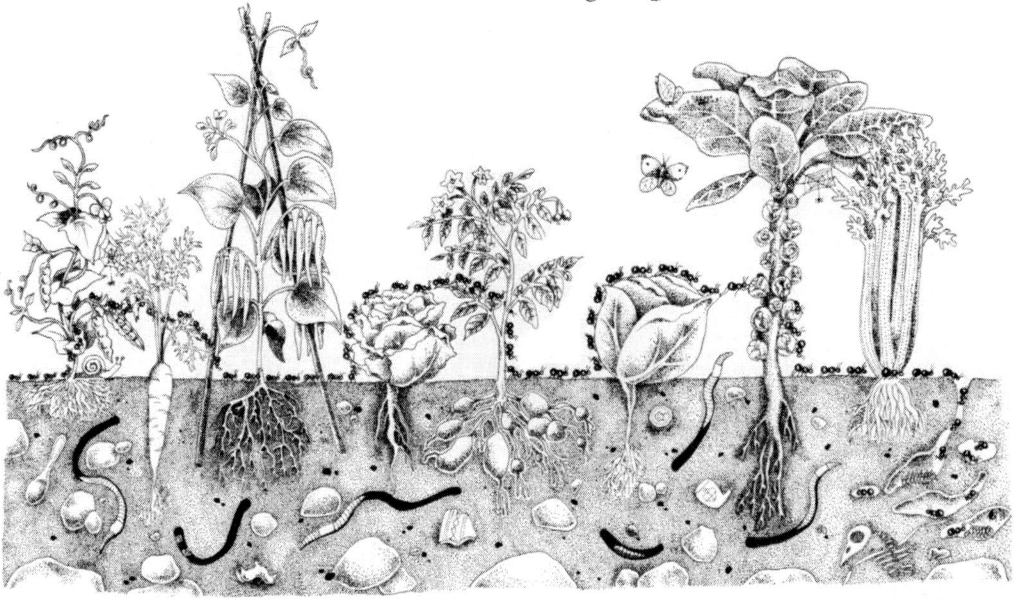

And what is more, Farmer Mack let it be known that he would do
the same every single year

- but he never grew turnips again.

TURNIP FIELD

43

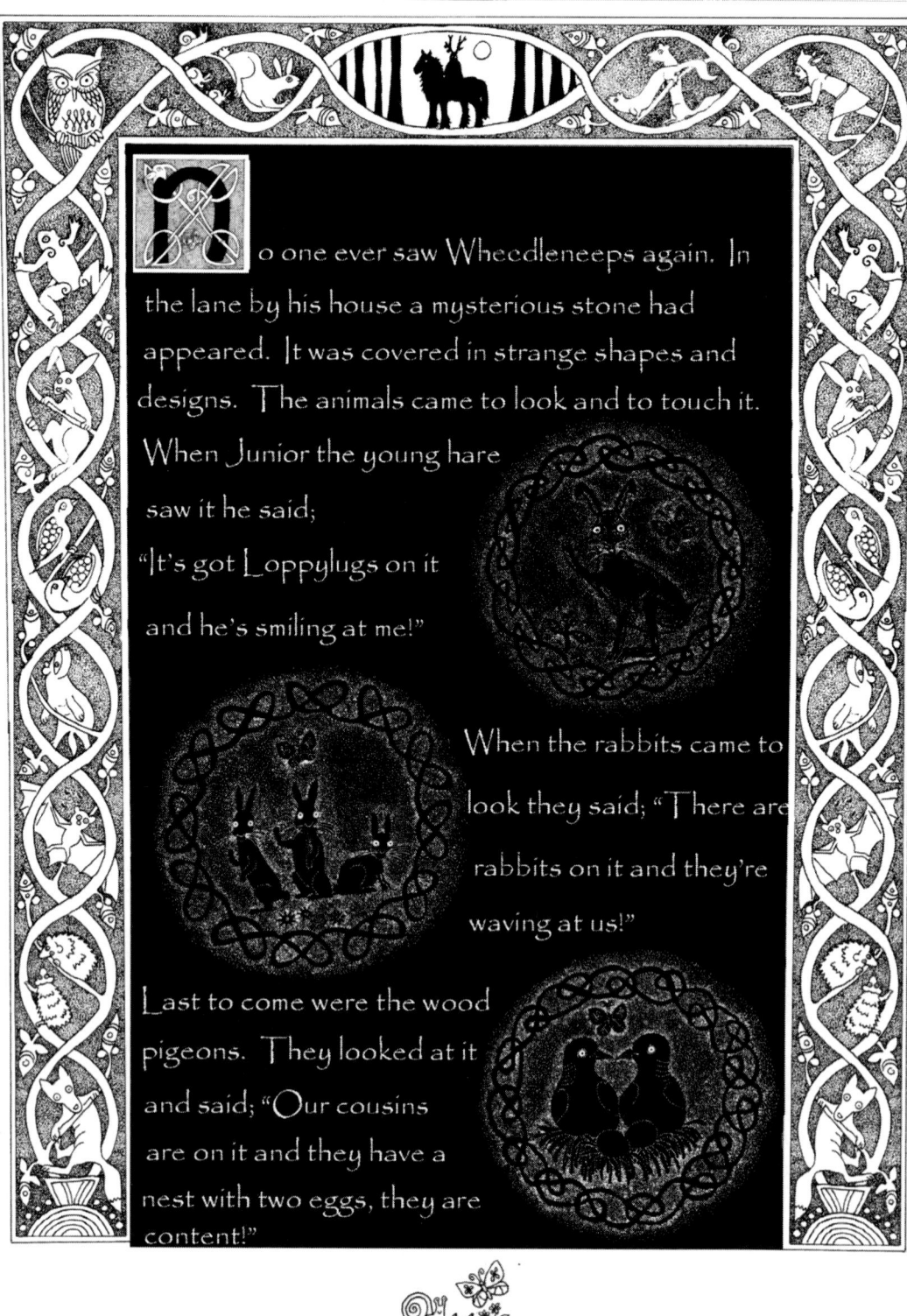

No one ever saw Wheedleneeps again. In the lane by his house a mysterious stone had appeared. It was covered in strange shapes and designs. The animals came to look and to touch it. When Junior the young hare saw it he said; "It's got Loppylugs on it and he's smiling at me!"

When the rabbits came to look they said; "There are rabbits on it and they're waving at us!"

Last to come were the wood pigeons. They looked at it and said; "Our cousins are on it and they have a nest with two eggs, they are content!"

One day you may pass the stone. It stands for all to see.
I saw it one night, just as it was getting dark. I saw the rabbits, the
hare and the pigeons. They were all sitting in the arms of a
Brownie with a bag of turnips at his feet.

And, as for Herne, yes, he still lives.

He is the Spirit of the Woodland, protector of all wild animals and it will always be so.

Remember him when you see the rainbow.

the end

46

Sandy McKnight is known locally as the tattooed poet. This is because he has loads of awesome tattoos and because he is an excellent poet. Originally hailing from Girvan in Ayrshire he now lives in the Rhins of Galloway where he makes wands and staffs and, when his neighbours are out, practices African Drumming. This is his first children's book, but he has lots more adventures in mind for Wheedleneeps!

Shalla Gray is not known locally as the tattooed poet. This is because her poetry is decidedly iffy and she only has one weeny tattoo. It is of a unicorn though, so bonus points there. Shalla lives in Galloway where she spends her free time ~~feeling very tired~~ ~~eating cake~~ ~~doing paperwork~~ ~~flaring her nostrils~~ ~~moaning~~ dancing with her pet unicorn Jeff.
She has written and illustrated several children's books but sadly not one with a unicorn in it (yet).

ISBN: 978-1-9996336-0-8

Published by Curly Tale Books Limited
34 Main Street
Kirkcowan
Newton Stewart
Dumfries & Galloway
DG8 0HG
www.curlytalebooks.co.uk

Also from Curly Tale Books...

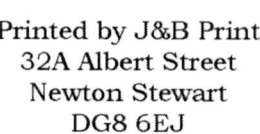

Printed by J&B Print
32A Albert Street
Newton Stewart
DG8 6EJ